A PREDICTABLE WORD BOOK

FREDDY THE FROG

Story by Janie Spaht Gill, Ph.D.
Illustrations by Bob Reese

ARO PUBLISHING

Freddy the Frog
jumped on a log.

5

The log sank,
he jumped on a bank.

The bank was steep,

he jumped in a jeep.

The jeep went fast,

he jumped in the grass.

The grass was tall,
he jumped on a wall.

14

The wall was big,
he jumped on a twig.

The twig was bent,
he jumped in a tent.

The tent was round,

he jumped on a clown.

The clown bowed,
he jumped in the crowd.

The crowd ran away,

so Freddy spent the day.